RAGGEDY ANN STORIES

RAGGEDY ANN
STORIES

Written & Illustrated by
JOHNNY GRUELLE

A YEARLING BOOK

Published by
DELL PUBLISHING CO., INC.
1 Dag Hammarskjold Plaza
New York, New York 10017

Yearling ® TM 913705, Dell Publishing Co., Inc.

ISBN: 0-440-47388-8

Reprinted by arrangement with The Bobbs-Merrill Company, Inc.

Printed in the United States of America

First Yearling printing—August 1977

PREFACE AND DEDICATION

As I write this, I have before me on my desk, propped up against the telephone, an old rag doll. Dear old Raggedy Ann!

The same Raggedy Ann with which my mother played when a child.

There she sits, a trifle loppy and loose-jointed, looking me squarely in the face in a straightforward, honest manner, a twinkle where her shoe-button eyes reflect the light.

Evidently Raggedy has been to a "tea party" today, for her face is covered with chocolate.

She smiles happily and continuously.

True, she has been nibbled by mice, who have made nests out of the soft cotton with which she has been stuffed, but Raggedy smiled just as broadly when the mice nibbled at her, for her smile is painted on.

What adventures you must have had, Raggedy!

What joy and happiness you have brought into this world!

And no matter what treatment you have received, how patient you have been!

What lessons of kindness and fortitude you might teach could you but talk; you with your wisdom of fifty-nine years. No wonder Rag Dolls are the best beloved! You are so kindly, so patient, so lovable.

The more you become torn, tattered and loose-jointed, Rag Dolls, the more you are loved by children.

Who knows but that Fairyland is filled with old, lovable Rag Dolls—soft, loppy Rag Dolls who ride through all the wonders of Fairyland in the crook of dimpled arms, snuggling close to childish breasts within which beat hearts filled with eternal sunshine.

So, to the millions of children and grown-ups who have loved a Rag Doll, I dedicate these stories of Raggedy Ann.

JOHNNY GRUELLE.

INTRODUCTION

Marcella liked to play up in the attic at Grandma's quaint old house, 'way out in the country, for there were so many old forgotten things to find up there.

One day when Marcella was up in the attic and had played with the old spinning wheel until she had grown tired of it, she curled up on an old horse-hair sofa to rest.

"I wonder what is in that barrel, 'way back in the corner?" she thought, as she jumped from the sofa and climbed over two dusty trunks to the barrel standing back under the eaves.

It was quite dark back there, so when Marcella had pulled a large bundle of things from the barrel she took them over to the dormer window where she could see better. There was a funny little bonnet with long white ribbons. Marcella put it on.

In an old leather bag she found a number of tin-types of queer looking men and women in old-fashioned clothes. And there was one picture of a very pretty little girl with long curls tied tightly back from her forehead and wearing a long dress and queer pantaloons which reached to her shoe-tops. And then out of the heap she pulled an old rag doll with only one shoe-button eye and a painted nose and a smiling mouth. Her dress was of soft material, blue with pretty little flowers and dots all over it.

Forgetting everything else in the happiness of her find, Marcella caught up the rag doll and ran downstairs to show it to Grandma.

"Well! Well! Where did you find it?" Grandma cried. "It's old Raggedy Ann!" she went on as she hugged the doll to her breast. "I had forgotten her. She has been in the attic for fifty years, I guess! Well! Well! Dear old Raggedy Ann! I will sew another button on her right away!" and Grandma went to the machine drawer and got her needle and thread.

Marcella watched the sewing while Grandma told how she had played with Raggedy Ann when she was a little girl.

"Now!" Grandma laughed, "Raggedy Ann, you have two fine shoe-button eyes and with them you can see the changes that have taken place in the world while you have been shut up so long in the attic! For, Raggedy Ann, you have a new playmate and mistress now, and I hope you both will have as much happiness together as you and I used to have!"

Then Grandma gave Raggedy Ann to Marcella, saying very seriously, "Marcella, let me introduce my very dear friend, Raggedy Ann. Raggedy, this is my granddaughter, Marcella!" And Grandma gave the doll a twitch with her fingers in such a way that the rag doll nodded her head to Marcella.

"Oh, Grandma! Thank you ever and ever so much!" Marcella cried as she gave Grandma a hug and kiss. "Raggedy Ann and I will have just loads of fun."

And this is how Raggedy Ann joined the doll family at Marcella's house, where she began the adventures of Raggedy Ann, told in the following stories.

RAGGEDY ANN LEARNS A LESSON

One day the dolls were left all to themselves.

Their little mistress had placed them all around the room and told them to be nice children while she was away.

And there they sat and never even so much as wiggled a finger, until their mistress had left the room.

Then the soldier dolly turned his head and solemnly winked at Raggedy Ann.

And when the front gate clicked and the dollies knew they were alone, they all scrambled to their feet.

"Now let's have a good time!" cried the tin soldier. "Let's all go in search of something to eat!"

"Yes! Let's all go in search of something to eat!" cried all the other dollies.

"When Mistress had me out playing with me this morning," said Raggedy Ann, "she carried me by a door near the back of the house and I smelled something which smelled as if it would taste delicious!"

"Then you lead the way, Raggedy Ann!" cried the French dolly.

"I think it would be a good plan to elect Raggedy Ann as our leader on this expedition!" said the Indian doll.

At this all the other dolls clapped their hands together and shouted, "Hurrah! Raggedy Ann will be our leader."

So Raggedy Ann, very proud indeed to have the confidence and love of all the other dollies, said that she would be very glad to be their leader.

"Follow me!" she cried as her wobbly legs carried her across the floor at a lively pace.

The other dollies followed, racing about the house until they came to the pantry door. "This is the place!" cried Raggedy Ann, and sure enough, all the dollies smelled something which they knew must be very good to eat.

But none of the dollies was tall enough to open the door and, although they pushed and pulled with all their might, the door remained tightly closed.

The dollies were talking and pulling and pushing and every once in a while one would fall over and the others would step on her in their efforts to open the door. Finally Raggedy Ann drew away and sat down on the floor.

When the other dollies discovered Raggedy Ann sitting there, running her rag hands through her yarn hair, they knew she was thinking.

"Sh! Sh!" they said to each other and quietly went over near Raggedy Ann and sat down in front of her.

"There must be a way!" said Raggedy Ann.

"Raggedy says there must be a way to get inside!" cried all the dolls.

"I can't seem to think clearly to-day," said Raggedy Ann. "It feels as if my head were ripped."

At this the French doll ran to Raggedy Ann and took off her bonnet. "Yes, there is a rip in your head, Raggedy!" she said and pulled a pin from her skirt and pinned up Raggedy's head. "It's not a very neat job, for I got some puckers in it!" she said.

"Oh that is ever so much better!" cried Raggedy Ann. "Now I can think quite clearly."

"Now Raggedy can think clearly!" cried all the dolls.

"My thoughts must have leaked out the rip before!" said Raggedy Ann.

"They must have leaked out before, dear Raggedy!" cried all the other dolls.

14

"Now that I can think so clearly," said Raggedy Ann, "I think the door must be locked and to get in we must unlock it!"

"That will be easy!" said the Dutch doll who says "Mamma" when he is tipped backward and forward, "For the brave tin soldier can shoot the key out of the lock!"

"I can easily do that!" cried the tin soldier, as he raised his gun.

"Oh, Raggedy Ann!" cried the French dolly, "Please do not let him shoot!"

"No!" said Raggedy Ann, "We must think of a quieter way!"

After thinking quite hard for a moment, Raggedy Ann jumped up and said: "I have it!" And she caught up the Jumping Jack and held

him up to the door; then Jack slid up his stick and unlocked the door.

Then the dollies all pushed and the door swung open.

My! Such a scramble! The dolls piled over one another in their desire to be the first at the goodies.

They swarmed upon the pantry shelves and in their eagerness spilled a pitcher of cream which ran all over the French dolly's dress.

The Indian doll found some corn bread and dipping it in the molasses he sat down for a good feast.

A jar of raspberry jam was overturned and

the dollies ate of this until their faces were all purple.

The tin soldier fell from the shelf three times and bent one of his tin legs, but he scrambled right back up again.

Never had the dolls had so much fun and excitement, and they had all eaten their fill when they heard the click of the front gate.

They did not take time to climb from the shelves, but all rolled or jumped off to the floor and scrambled back to their room as fast as they could run, leaving a trail of bread crumbs and jam along the way back to the nursery.

Just as their mistress came into the room the dolls dropped in whatever positions they happened to be in.

"This is funny!" cried Mistress. "They were all left sitting in their places around the room! I wonder if Fido has been shaking them up!" Then she saw Raggedy Ann's face and picked her up. "Why Raggedy Ann, you are all sticky! I do believe you are covered with jam!" and Mistress tasted Raggedy Ann's hand. "Yes! It's JAM! Shame on you, Raggedy Ann! You've been in the pantry and all the others, too!" and with this the doll's mistress dropped Raggedy Ann on the floor and left the room.

When she came back she had on an apron and her sleeves were rolled up.

She picked up all the sticky dolls and putting them in a basket she carried them out under the apple tree in the garden.

There she placed her little tub and wringer and she took the dolls one at a time, and scrubbed them with a scrubbing brush and soused them up and down and this way and that in the soap suds until they were clean.

Then she hung them all out on the clothes-line in the sunshine to dry.

There the dolls hung all day, swinging and twisting about as the breeze swayed the clothes-line.

"I do believe she scrubbed my face so hard she wore off my smile!" said Raggedy Ann, after an hour of silence.

"No, it is still there!" said the tin soldier, as the wind twisted him around so he could see Raggedy. "But I do believe my arms will never work without squeaking, they feel so rusted," he added.

Just then the wind twisted the little Dutch doll and loosened his clothes-pin, so that he fell to the grass below with a sawdusty bump and as he rolled over he said, "Mamma!" in a squeaky voice.

Late in the afternoon the back door opened and the little mistress came out with a table and chairs. After setting the table she took all the dolls from the line and placed them about the table.

They had lemonade with grape jelly in it, which made it a beautiful lavender color, and little "Baby-teeny-weeny-cookies" with powdered sugar on them.

After this lovely dinner, the dollies were taken in the house, where they had their hair brushed and nice clean nighties put on.

Then they were placed in their beds and Mistress kissed each one good night and tiptoed from the room closing the door very gently behind her.

All the dolls lay as still as mice for a few minutes, then Raggedy Ann raised upon her cotton-stuffed elbows and said: "I have been thinking!"

"Sh!" said all the other dollies, "Raggedy has been thinking!"

"Yes," said Raggedy Ann, "I have been thinking; our mistress gave us the nice dinner out under the trees to teach us a lesson. She wanted to teach us that we could have had all the goodies we wished, if we had behaved ourselves. And our lesson was that we must never take without asking what we could always have for the asking! So let us all remember and try never again to do anything which might cause those who love us any unhappiness of any kind!"

"Let us all remember," chimed all the other dollies.

And Raggedy Ann, with a merry twinkle in her shoe-button eyes, lay back in her little bed, her cotton head filled with thoughts of love and happiness.

RAGGEDY ANN AND
THE WASHING

"Why, Dinah! How could you!"

Mamma looked out of the window and saw Marcella run up to Dinah and take something out of her hand and start to cry.

"What is the trouble, Dear?" Mamma asked, as she came out the door and knelt beside the little figure shaking with sobs.

Marcella held out Raggedy Ann. But such a comical looking Raggedy Ann!

Mamma had to smile in spite of her sympathy, for Raggedy Ann looked ridiculous!

Dinah's big eyes rolled about in a troubled manner, for Marcella had snatched Raggedy Ann from Dinah's hand as she cried, "Why, Dinah! How could you?"

Dinah could not quite understand and, as she dearly loved Marcella, she was troubled.

Raggedy Ann was not in the least down-hearted and while she felt she must look very funny she continued to smile, but with a more expansive smile than ever before.

Raggedy Ann knew just how it all happened and her remaining shoe-button eye twinkled.

She remembered that morning when Marcella came to the nursery to take the nighties from the dolls and dress them she had been cross.

Raggedy Ann thought at the time, "Perhaps she had climbed out of bed backwards!" For Marcella complained to each doll as she dressed them.

And when it came Raggedy's time to be dressed, Marcella was very cross for she had scratched her finger on a pin when dressing the French doll.

So, when Marcella heard the little girl next door calling to her, she ran out of the nursery and gave Raggedy Ann a toss from her as she ran.

Now it happened Raggedy lit in the clothes hamper and there she lay all doubled up in a knot.

A few minutes afterwards Dinah came through the hall with an armful of clothes and piled them in the hamper on top of Raggedy Ann.

Then Dinah carried the hamper out in back of the house where she did the washing.

Dinah dumped all the clothes into the boiler and poured water on them.

The boiler was then placed upon the stove.

When the water began to get warm, Raggedy Ann wiggled around and climbed up amongst the clothes to the top of the boiler to peek out. There was too much steam and she could see nothing. For that matter, Dinah could not see Raggedy Ann, either, on account of the steam.

So Dinah, using an old broom handle, stirred the clothes in the boiler and the clothes and Raggedy Ann were whirled around until all were thoroughly boiled.

When Dinah took the clothes a piece at a time

from the boiler, she finally came upon Raggedy Ann.

Now Dinah did not know but that Marcella had placed Raggedy in the clothes hamper to be washed, so she soaped Raggedy well and rubbed her up and down the wash-board.

Two buttons from the back of Raggedy's dress came off and one of Raggedy Ann's shoe-button eyes was loosened as Dinah gave her face a final scrub down the wash-board.

Then Dinah put Raggedy Ann's feet in the wringer and turned the crank. It was hard work getting Raggedy through the wringer, but Dinah

was very strong. And of course it happened! Raggedy Ann came through as flat as a pancake.

It was just then Marcella returned and saw Raggedy.

"Why, Dinah! How could you!" Marcella had sobbed as she snatched the flattened Raggedy Ann from the bewildered Dinah's hand.

Mamma patted Marcella's hand and soon coaxed her to quit sobbing.

When Dinah explained that the first she knew of Raggedy being in the wash was when she took her from the boiler. Marcella began crying again.

"It was all my fault, Mamma!" she cried. "I remember now that I threw dear old Raggedy Ann from me as I ran out the door and she must have fallen in the clothes hamper! Oh dear! Oh dear!" and she hugged Raggedy Ann tight.

Mamma did not tell Marcella that she had been cross and naughty for she knew Marcella felt very sorry. Instead Mamma put her arms around her and said, "Just see how Raggedy Ann takes it! She doesn't seem to be unhappy!"

And when Marcella brushed her tears away and looked at Raggedy Ann, flat as a pancake and with a cheery smile upon her painted face, she had to laugh. And Mamma and Dinah had to laugh, too, for Raggedy Ann's smile was almost twice as broad as it had been before.

"Jess lemme hang Miss Raggedy on de line in de bright sunshine foh haff an hour," said Dinah, "an' you won't know her when she comes off!"

So Raggedy Ann was pinned to the clothesline, out in the sunshine, where she swayed and twisted in the breeze and listened to the chatter of the robins in a nearby tree.

Every once in a while Dinah went out and rolled and patted Raggedy until her cotton stuffing was soft and dry and fluffy and her head and arms and legs were nice and round again.

Then she took Raggedy Ann into the house and showed Marcella and Mamma how clean and sweet she was.

Marcella took Raggedy Ann right up to the nursery and told all the dolls just what had happened and how sorry she was that she had been so cross and peevish when she dressed them. And while the dolls said never a word they looked at their little mistress with love in their eyes as she sat in the little red rocking chair and held Raggedy Ann tightly in her arms.

And Raggedy Ann's remaining shoe-button eye looked up at her little mistress in rather a saucy manner, but upon her face was the same old smile of happiness, good humor and love.

RAGGEDY ANN AND THE KITE

Raggedy Ann watched with interest the preparations.

A number of sticks were being fastened together with strings and covered with light cloth.

Raggedy Ann heard some of the boys talk of "The Kite," so Raggedy Ann knew this must be a kite.

When a tail had been fastened to the kite and a large ball of heavy twine tied to the front, one of the boys held the kite up in the air and another boy walked off, unwinding the ball of twine.

There was a nice breeze blowing, so the boy with the twine called, "Let 'er go!" and started running.

Marcella held Raggedy up so that she could watch.

How nicely it climbed! But suddenly the kite

acted strangely, and as all the children shouted advice to the boy with the ball of twine, the kite began darting this way and that, and finally making four or five loop-the-loops, it crashed to the ground.

"It needs more tail on it!" one boy shouted.

Then the children asked each other where they might get more rags to fasten to the tail of the kite.

"Let's tie Raggedy Ann to the tail!" suggested Marcella. "I know she would enjoy a trip way up in the sky!"

The boys all shouted with delight at this new suggestion. So Raggedy Ann was tied to the tail of the kite.

This time the kite rose straight in the air and remained steady. The ball of twine unwound until the kite and Raggedy Ann were 'way, 'way up and far away. How Raggedy Ann enjoyed being up there! She could see for miles and miles! And how tiny the children looked!

Suddenly a great puff of wind came and carried Raggedy Ann streaming way out behind the kite! She could hear the wind singing on the twine as the strain increased.

Suddenly Raggedy Ann felt something rip. It was the rag to which she was tied. As each puff of wind caught her the rip widened.

When Marcella watched Raggedy Ann rise

high above the field, she wondered how much Raggedy Ann enjoyed it, and wished that she, too, might have gone along. But after the kite had been up in the air for five or ten minutes, Marcella grew restless. Kites were rather tiresome. There was more fun in tea parties out under the apple tree.

"Will you please pull down the kite now?" she asked the boy with the twine. "I want Raggedy Ann."

"Let her ride up there!" the boy replied. "We'll bring her home when we pull down the kite! We're going to get another ball of twine and let her go higher!"

Marcella did not like to leave Raggedy Ann with the boys, so she sat down upon the ground to wait until they pulled down the kite.

But while Marcella watched Raggedy Ann, a dot in the sky, she could not see the wind ripping the rag to which Raggedy was tied.

Suddenly the rag parted and Raggedy Ann went sailing away as the wind caught in her skirts.

Marcella jumped from the ground, too surprised to say anything. The kite, released from the weight of Raggedy Ann began darting and swooping to the ground.

"We'll get her for you!" some of the boys said when they saw Marcella's troubled face, and they started running in the direction Raggedy Ann had fallen. Marcella and the other girls ran with

them. They ran, and they ran, and they ran, and at last they found the kite upon the ground with one of the sticks broken, but they could not find Raggedy Ann anywhere.

"She must have fallen almost in your yard!" a boy said to Marcella, "for the kite was directly over here when the doll fell!"

Marcella was heartbroken. She went in the house and lay on the bed. Mamma went out with the children and tried to find Raggedy Ann, but Raggedy Ann was nowhere to be seen.

When Daddy came home in the evening he tried to find Raggedy, but met with no success. Marcella had eaten hardly any dinner, nor could she be comforted by Mamma or Daddy. The other dolls in the nursery lay forgotten and were not put to bed that night, for Marcella lay and sobbed and tossed about her bed.

Finally she said a little prayer for Raggedy Ann, and went to sleep. And as she slept Marcella dreamed that the fairies came and took Raggedy Ann with them to fairyland for a visit, and then sent Raggedy Ann home to her. She awakened with a cry. Of course Mamma came to her bed right away and said that Daddy would offer a reward in the morning for the return of Raggedy.

"It was all my fault, Mamma!" Marcella said. "I should not have offered the boys dear old

Raggedy Ann to tie on the tail of the kite! But I just know the fairies will send her back."

Mamma took her in her arms and soothed her with cheering words, although she felt indeed that Raggedy Ann was truly lost and would never be found again.

Now, where do you suppose Raggedy Ann was all this time?

When Raggedy Ann dropped from the kite, the wind caught in her skirts and carried her along until she fell in the fork of the large elm tree directly over Marcella's house. When Raggedy Ann fell with a thud, face up in the fork of the tree, two robins who had a nest near by flew chattering away.

Presently the robins returned and quarreled at Raggedy Ann for lying so close to their nest, but Raggedy Ann only smiled at them and did not move.

When the robins quieted down and quit their quarreling, one of them hopped up closer to Raggedy Ann in order to investigate.

It was Mamma Robin. She called to Daddy Robin and told him to come. "See the nice yarn! We could use it to line the nest with," she said.

So the robins hopped close to Raggedy Ann and asked if they might have some of her yarn hair to line their nests. Raggedy Ann smiled at them. So the two robins pulled and tugged at Raggedy Ann's yarn hair until they had enough to line their nest nice and soft.

Evening came and the robins sang their good night songs, and Raggedy Ann watched the stars come out, twinkle all night and disappear in the morning light. In the morning the robins again pulled yarn from Raggedy Ann's head, and loosened her so she could peep over the side of the limb, and when the sun came up Raggedy Ann saw she was in the trees in her own yard.

Now before she could eat any breakfast, Marcella started out to find Raggedy Ann. And it was Marcella herself who found her. And this is how she did it.

Mamma Robin had seen Marcella with Raggedy Ann out in the yard many times, so she began calling "Cheery! Cheery!" and Daddy Robin started calling "Cheery! Cheery! Cheer up! Cheer up! Cheerily! Cheerily! Cheery! Cheery!" And Marcella looking up into the tree above the house to see the robins, discovered Raggedy Ann peeping over the limb at her.

Oh, how her heart beat with happiness. "Here is Raggedy Ann," she shouted as she ran toward the house.

And Mamma and Daddy came out and saw Raggedy smiling at them, and Daddy got the clothes prop and climbed out of the attic window and poked Raggedy Ann out of the tree and she fell right into Marcella's arms where she was hugged in a tight embrace.

"You'll never go up on a kite again, Raggedy Ann!" said Marcella, "for I felt so lost without you. I will never let you leave me again."

So Raggedy Ann went into the house and had breakfast with her little mistress and Mamma and Daddy smiled at each other when they peeped through the door into the breakfast room, for Raggedy Ann's smile was wide and very yellow. Marcella, her heart full of happiness, was feeding Raggedy Ann part of her egg.

RAGGEDY ANN RESCUES FIDO

It was almost midnight and the dolls were asleep in their beds; all except Raggedy Ann.

Raggedy lay there, her shoe-button eyes staring straight up at the ceiling. Every once in a while Raggedy Ann ran her rag hand up through her yarn hair. She was thinking.

When she had thought for a long, long time, Raggedy Ann raised herself on her wobbly elbows and said, "I've thought it all out."

At this the other dolls shook each other and raised up saying, "Listen! Raggedy has thought it all out!"

"Tell us what you have been thinking, dear Raggedy," said the tin soldier. "We hope they were pleasant thoughts."

"Not very pleasant thoughts!" said Raggedy, as she brushed a tear from her shoe-button eyes.

"You haven't seen Fido all day, have you?"

"Not since early this morning," the French dolly said.

"It has troubled me," said Raggedy, "and if my head was not stuffed with lovely new white cotton, I am sure it would have ached with the worry! When Mistress took me into the living-room this afternoon she was crying, and I heard her mamma say, 'We will find him! He is sure to come home soon!' and I knew they were talking of Fido! He must be lost!"

The tin soldier jumped out of bed and ran over to Fido's basket, his tin feet clicking on the floor as he went. "He is not here," he said.

"When I was sitting in the window about noon-time," said the Indian doll, "I saw Fido and a yellow scraggly dog playing out on the lawn and they ran out through a hole in the fence!"

"That was Priscilla's dog, Peterkins!" said the French doll.

"I know poor Mistress is very sad on account of Fido," said the Dutch doll, "Because I was in the dining-room at supper-time and I heard her daddy tell her to eat her supper and he would go out and find Fido; but I had forgotten all about it until now."

"That is the trouble with all of us except Raggedy Ann!" cried the little penny doll, in a squeaky voice, "She has to think for all of us!"

"I think it would be a good plan for us to

44

show our love for Mistress and try and find Fido!" exclaimed Raggedy.

"It is a good plan, Raggedy Ann!" cried all the dolls.

"Then let us waste no more time in talking!" said Raggedy Ann, as she jumped from bed, followed by the rest.

The nursery window was open, so the dolls helped each other up on the sill and then jumped to the soft grass below. They fell in all sorts of queer attitudes, but of course the fall did not hurt them.

At the hole in the fence the Indian doll picked up the trail of the two dogs, and the dolls, stringing out behind, followed him until they came to Peterkins' house. Peterkins was surprised to see the strange little figures in white nighties come stringing up the path to the dog house.

Peterkins was too large to sleep in the nursery, so he had a nice cozy dog-house under the grape arbor.

"Come in," Peterkins said when he saw and recognized the dolls, so all the dollies went into Peterkins' house and sat about while Raggedy told him why they had come.

"It has worried me, too!" said Peterkins, "but I had no way of telling your mistress where Fido was, for she cannot understand dog language! For you see," Peterkins continued, "Fido and I were having the grandest romp over in the park

45

when a great big man with a funny thing on the end of a stick came running towards us. We barked at him and Fido thought he was trying to play with us and went up too close and do you know, that wicked man caught Fido in the thing at the end of the stick and carried him to a wagon and dumped him in with a lot of other dogs!"

"*The Dog Catcher!*" cried Raggedy Ann.

"Yes!" said Peterkins, as he wiped his eyes with his paws. "It was the dog catcher! For I followed the wagon at a distance and I saw him put all the dogs into a big wire pen, so that none could get out!"

"Then you know the way there, Peterkins?" asked Raggedy Ann.

"Yes, I can find it easily," Peterkins said.

"Then show us the way!" Raggedy Ann cried, "for we must try to rescue Fido."

So Peterkins led the way up alleys and across streets, the dolls all pattering along behind him. It was a strange procession. Once a strange dog ran out at them, but Peterkins told him to mind his own business and the strange dog returned to his own yard.

At last they came to the dog catcher's place. Some of the dogs in the pen were barking at the moon and others were whining and crying.

There was Fido, all covered with mud, and his pretty red ribbon dragging on the ground. My,

but he was glad to see the dolls and Peterkins! All the dogs came to the side of the pen and twisted their heads from side to side, gazing in wonder at the queer figures of the dolls.

"We will try and let you out," said Raggedy Ann.

At this all the dogs barked joyfully.

Then Raggedy Ann, the other dolls and Peterkins went to the gate.

The catch was too high for Raggedy Ann to reach, but Peterkins held Raggedy Ann in his mouth and stood up on his hind legs so that she could raise the catch.

When the catch was raised, the dogs were so anxious to get out they pushed and jumped against the gate so hard it flew open, knocking Peterkins and Raggedy Ann into the mud. Such a yapping and barking was never heard in the neighborhood as when the dogs swarmed out of the enclosure, jumping over one another and scrambling about in the mad rush out the gate.

Fido picked himself up from where he had been rolled by the large dogs and helped Raggedy Ann to her feet. He, Peterkins, and all the dolls ran after the pack of dogs, turning the corner just as the dog catcher came running out of the house in his nightgown to see what was causing the trouble.

He stopped in astonishment when he saw the string of dolls in white nighties pattering down the alley, for he could not imagine what they were.

Well, you may be sure the dolls thanked Peterkins for his kind assistance and they and Fido ran on home, for a faint light was beginning to show in the east where the sun was getting ready to come up.

When they got to their own home they found an old chair out in the yard and after a great deal of work they finally dragged it to the window and thus managed to get into the nursery again.

Fido was very grateful to Raggedy Ann and the other dolls and before he went to his basket he gave them each a lick on the cheek.

The dolls lost no time in scrambling into bed and pulling up the covers, for they were very sleepy, but just as they were dozing off, Raggedy Ann raised herself and said, "If my legs and arms were not stuffed with nice clean cotton I feel sure they would ache, but being stuffed with nice clean white cotton, they do not ache and I could not feel happier if my body were stuffed with sunshine, for I know how pleased and happy Mistress will be in the morning when she discovers Fido asleep in his own little basket, safe and sound at home."

And as the dollies by this time were all asleep, Raggedy Ann pulled the sheet up to her chin and smiled so hard she ripped two stitches out of the back of her rag head.

RAGGEDY ANN
AND THE PAINTER

When housecleaning time came around, Mistress'
mamma decided that she would have the nursery
repainted and new paper put upon the walls.
That was why all the dolls happened to be laid
helter-skelter upon one of the high shelves.

Mistress had been in to look at them and
wished to put them to bed, but as the painters
were coming again in the early morning, Mamma
thought it best that their beds be piled in the
closet.

When all was quiet that night, Raggedy Ann
who was on the bottom of the pile of dolls spoke
softly and asked the others if they would mind
moving along the shelf.

"The cotton in my body is getting mashed as

flat as a pancake!" said Raggedy Ann. And although the tin soldier was piled so that his foot was pressed into Raggedy's face, she still wore her customary smile.

So the dolls began moving off to one side until Raggedy Ann was free to sit up.

"Ah, that's a great deal better!" she said, stretching her arms and legs and patting her dress into shape.

"Well, I'll be glad when morning comes!" she said finally, "For I know Mistress will take us out in the yard and play with us under the trees, and we may have a party."

So the dolls sat and talked until daylight, when the painters came to work.

One of the painters, a young fellow, seeing the dolls, reached up and took Raggedy Ann down from the shelf.

"Look at this rag doll, Jim," he said to one of the other painters, "She's a daisy," and he took Raggedy Ann by the hands and danced with her while he whistled a lively tune. Raggedy Ann's heels hit the floor thumpity-thump and she enjoyed it immensely.

The other dolls sat upon the shelf and looked straight before them, for it would never do to let grown-up men know that dolls were really alive.

"Better put her back upon the shelf," said one of the other men. "You'll have the little girl after

you! The chances are that she likes that old rag doll better than any of the others!"

But the young painter twisted Raggedy Ann into funny attitudes and laughed and laughed as she looped about. Finally he got to tossing her up in the air and catching her. This was great fun for Raggedy and as she sailed up by the shelf the dolls all smiled at her, for it pleased them whenever Raggedy Ann was happy.

But the young fellow threw Raggedy Ann up into the air once too often and when she came down he failed to catch her and she came down *splash*, head first into a bucket of oily paint.

"I told you!" said the older painter, "and now you are in for it!"

"My goodness! I didn't mean to do it!" said the young fellow, "What had I better do with her?"

"Better put her back on the shelf!" replied the other.

So Raggedy was placed back upon the shelf and the paint ran from her head and trickled down upon her dress.

After breakfast, Mistress came into the nursery and saw Raggedy all covered with paint and she began crying.

The young painter felt sorry and told her how it had happened.

"If you will let me," he said, "I will take her

home with me and will clean her up tonight and will bring her back day after tomorrow."

So Raggedy was wrapped in a newspaper that evening and carried away.

All the dolls felt sad that night without Raggedy Ann near them.

"Poor Raggedy! I could have cried when I saw her all covered with paint!" said the French doll.

"She didn't look like our dear old Raggedy Ann at all!" said the tin soldier, who wiped the tears from his eyes so that they would not run down on his arms and rust them.

"The paint covered her lovely smile and nose and you could not see the laughter in her shoe-button eyes!" said the Indian doll.

And so the dolls talked that night and the next.

But in the daytime when the painters were there, they kept very quiet.

The second day Raggedy was brought home and the dolls were all anxious for night to come so that they could see and talk with Raggedy Ann.

At last the painters left and the house was quiet, for Mistress had been in and placed Raggedy on the shelf with the other dolls.

"Tell us all about it, Raggedy dear!" the dolls cried.

"Oh I am so glad I fell in the paint!" cried Raggedy, after she had hugged all the dolls, "For

I have had the happiest time. The painter took me home and told his Mamma how I happened to be covered with paint and she was very sorry. She took a rag and wiped off my shoe-button eyes and then I saw that she was a very pretty, sweet-faced lady and she got some gasoline and wiped off most of the paint on my face.

"But you know," Raggedy continued, "the paint had soaked through my rag head and had made the cotton inside all sticky and soggy and I could not think clearly. And my yarn hair was all matted with paint.

"So the kind lady took off my yarn hair and cut the stitches out of my head and took out all the painty cotton.

"It was a great relief, although it felt queer at first and my thoughts seemed scattered.

"She left me in her work-basket that night and hung me out upon the clothes-line the next morning when she had washed the last of the paint off.

"And while I hung out on the clothes-line, what do you think?"

"We could never guess!" all the dolls cried.

"Why a dear little Jenny Wren came and picked enough cotton out of me to make a cute little cuddly nest in the grape arbor!"

"Wasn't that sweet!" cried all the dolls.

"Yes indeed it was!" replied Raggedy Ann,

"It made me very happy. Then when the lady took me in the house again she stuffed me with lovely nice new cotton, all the way from my knees up and sewed me up and put new yarn on my head for hair and—and—and it's a secret!" said Raggedy Ann.

"Oh tell us the secret!" cried all the dolls, as they pressed closer to Raggedy. "Well, I know you will not tell anyone who would not be glad to know about it, so I will tell you the secret and why I am wearing my smile a trifle broader!" said Raggedy Ann.

The dolls all said that Raggedy Ann's smile was indeed a quarter of an inch wider on each side.

"When the dear lady put the new white cotton in my body," said Raggedy Ann, "she went to the cupboard and came back with a paper bag. And she took from the bag ten or fifteen little candy hearts with mottoes on them and she hunted through the candy hearts until she found a beautiful red one which she sewed up in me with the cotton! So that is the secret, and that is why I am so happy! Feel here," said Raggedy Ann. All the dolls could feel Raggedy Ann's beautiful new candy heart and they were very happy for her.

After all had hugged each other good night and had cuddled up for the night, the tin soldier asked, "Did you have a chance to see what the motto on your new candy heart was, Raggedy Ann?"

"Oh yes," replied Raggedy Ann, "I was so happy I forgot to tell you. It had printed upon it in nice blue letters, 'I LOVE YOU.'"

RAGGEDY ANN'S
TRIP ON THE RIVER

When Marcella had a tea party out in the orchard, of course all of the dolls were invited. Raggedy Ann, the tin soldier, the Indian doll and all the others—even the four little penny dolls in the spool box. After a lovely tea party with ginger cookies and milk, of course the dolls were very sleepy, at least Marcella thought so, so she took all except Raggedy Ann into the house and put them to bed for the afternoon nap. Then Marcella told Raggedy Ann to stay there and watch the things.

As there was nothing else to do, Raggedy Ann waited for Marcella to return. And as she watched the little ants eating cookie crumbs Marcella had thrown to them, she heard all of a sudden the patter of puppy feet behind her. It was Fido.

The puppy dog ran up to Raggedy Ann and twisted his head about as he looked at her. Then he put his front feet out and barked in Raggedy Ann's face. Raggedy Ann tried to look very stern, but she could not hide the broad smile painted on her face.

"Oh, you want to play, do you?" the puppy dog barked, as he jumped at Raggedy Ann and then jumped back again.

The more Raggedy Ann smiled, the livelier Fido's antics became, until finally he caught the end of her dress and dragged her about.

This was great fun for the puppy dog, but Raggedy Ann did not enjoy it. She kicked and twisted as much as she could, but the puppy dog thought Raggedy was playing.

He ran out the garden gate and down the path across the meadow. Every once in a while Fido would give Raggedy Ann a great shaking, making her yarn head hit the ground "ratty-tat-tat." Then he would give his head a toss and send Raggedy Ann high in the air.

By this time, she had lost her apron and now some of her yarn hair was coming loose.

As Fido neared the brook, another puppy dog came running across the foot-bridge to meet him. "What have you there, Fido?" said the new puppy dog as he bounced up to Raggedy Ann.

"This is Raggedy Ann," answered Fido. "She and I are having a lovely time playing."

You see, Fido really thought Raggedy enjoyed being tossed around and whirled high up in the air. But of course she didn't. However, the game didn't last much longer. As Raggedy Ann hit the ground the new puppy dog caught her dress and ran with her across the bridge, Fido barking close behind him.

In the center of the bridge, Fido caught up with the new puppy dog and they had a lively tug-of-war with Raggedy Ann stretched between them. As they pulled and tugged and flopped Raggedy Ann about, somehow she fell over the side of the bridge into the water.

The puppy dogs were surprised, and Fido was very sorry indeed, for he remembered how good Raggedy Ann had been to him and how she had rescued him from the dog-pound. But the current carried Raggedy Ann along and all Fido could do was to run along the bank and bark.

Now, you would have thought Raggedy Ann would sink, but no, she floated nicely, for she was stuffed with clean white cotton and the water didn't soak through very quickly.

After a while, the strange puppy and Fido grew tired of running along the bank and the strange puppy scampered home over the meadow, as if he had nothing to be ashamed of. But Fido walked home very sorry indeed. His little heart

was broken to think that he had caused Raggedy Ann to be drowned.

But Raggedy Ann didn't drown—not a bit of it. In fact, she even went to sleep on the brook, for the motion of the current was very soothing as it carried her along—just like being rocked by Marcella.

So, sleeping peacefully, Raggedy Ann drifted along until she lodged against a large stone.

Raggedy Ann tried to climb upon the stone, but by this time the water had thoroughly soaked through Raggedy Ann's nice, clean, white cotton stuffing and she was so heavy she could not climb.

So there she had to stay until Marcella and Daddy came along and found her.

You see, they had been looking for her. They

had found pieces of her apron all along the path where Fido and the strange puppy dog had shaken them from Raggedy Ann. So they followed the brook until they found her.

When Daddy fished Raggedy Ann from the water, Marcella hugged her so tightly to her breast the water ran from Raggedy Ann and dripped all over Marcella's apron. But Marcella was so glad to find Raggedy Ann again she didn't mind it a bit. She just hurried home and took off all of Raggedy Ann's wet clothes and placed her on a little red chair in front of the oven door, and then brought all of the other dolls in and read a fairy tale to them while Raggedy Ann steamed and dried.

When Raggedy Ann was thoroughly dry, Mamma said she thought the cake must be finished and she took from the oven a lovely chocolate cake and gave Marcella a large piece to have another tea party with.

That night when all the house was asleep, Raggedy Ann raised up in bed and said to the dolls who were still awake, "I am so happy I do not feel a bit sleepy. Do you know, I believe the water soaked me so thoroughly my candy heart must have melted and filled my whole body, and I do not feel the least bit angry with Fido for playing with me so roughly!"

So all the other dolls were happy, too, for happiness is very easy to catch when we love one another and are sweet all through.

RAGGEDY ANN
AND THE STRANGE DOLLS

Raggedy Ann lay just as Marcella had dropped her—all sprawled out with her rag arms and legs twisted in ungraceful attitudes.

Her yarn hair was twisted and lay partly over her face, hiding one of her shoe-button eyes.

Raggedy gave no sign that she had heard, but lay there smiling at the ceiling.

Perhaps Raggedy Ann knew that what the new dolls said was true.

But sometimes the truth may hurt and this may have been the reason Raggedy Ann lay there so still.

"Did you ever see such an ungainly creature!"

"I do believe it has shoe buttons for eyes!"

"And yarn hair!"

"Mercy, did you ever see such feet!"

The Dutch doll rolled off the doll sofa and said "Mamma" in his quavery voice, he was so surprised at hearing anyone speak so of beloved Raggedy Ann—she of the candy heart, whom all the dolls loved.

Uncle Clem was also very much surprised and offended. He walked up in front of the two new dolls and looked them sternly in the eyes, but he could think of nothing to say so he pulled at his yarn mustache.

Marcella received the two new dolls in the morning mail and they were presents from an aunt.

Marcella had named the two new dolls Annabel-Lee and Thomas, after her aunt and uncle.

Annabel-Lee and Thomas were beautiful dolls and must have cost heaps and heaps of shiny pennies, for both were handsomely dressed and had *real* hair!

Annabel's hair was of a lovely shade of auburn and Thomas' was golden yellow.

Annabel was dressed in soft, lace-covered silk and upon her head she wore a beautiful hat with long silk ribbons tied in a neat bow-knot beneath her dimpled chin.

Thomas was dressed in an Oliver Twist suit of dark velvet with a lace collar. Both he and Annabel wore lovely black slippers and short stockings.

They were sitting upon two of the little red

chairs where Marcella placed them so they could see the other dolls.

When Uncle Clem walked in front of them and pulled his mustache they laughed outright. "Tee-Hee-Hee!" they snickered, "He has holes in his knees!"

Quite true. Uncle Clem was made of worsted and the moths had eaten his knees and part of his kiltie. He had a kiltie, you see, for Uncle Clem was a Scotch doll.

Uncle Clem shook, but he felt so hurt he could think of nothing to say.

He walked over and sat down beside Raggedy Ann and brushed her yarn hair away from her shoe-button eye.

The tin soldier went over and sat beside them.

"Don't you mind what they say, Raggedy!" he said, "They do not know you as we do!"

"We don't care to know her!" said Annabel-Lee as she primped her dress, "She looks like a scarecrow!"

"And the Soldier must have been made with a can opener!" laughed Thomas.

"You should be ashamed of yourselves!" said the French dollie, as she stood before Annabel and Thomas, "You will make all of us sorry that you have joined our family if you continue to poke fun at us and look down upon us. We are all happy here together and share in each others' adventures and happiness."

Now, that night Marcella did not undress the two new dolls, for she had no nighties for them, so she let them sit up in the two little red doll chairs so they would not muss their clothes. "I will make nighties for you tomorrow!" she said as she kissed them good night. Then she went over and gave Raggedy Ann a good night hug.

"Take good care of all my children, Raggedy!" she said as she went out.

Annabel and Thomas whispered together, "Perhaps we have been too hasty in our judgment!" said Annabel-Lee. "This Raggedy Ann seems to be a favorite with the mistress and with all the dolls!"

"There must be a reason!" replied Thomas, "I am beginning to feel sorry that we spoke of her looks. One really cannot help one's looks after all."

Now, Annabel-Lee and Thomas were very tired after their long journey and soon they fell asleep and forgot all about the other dolls.

When they were sound asleep, Raggedy Ann slipped quietly from her bed and awakened the tin soldier and Uncle Clem and the three tiptoed to the two beautiful new dolls.

They lifted them gently so as not to awaken them and carried them to Raggedy Ann's bed.

Raggedy Ann tucked them in snugly and lay down upon the hard floor.

The tin soldier and Uncle Clem both tried to coax Raggedy Ann into accepting their bed (they slept together), but Raggedy Ann would not hear of it.

"I am stuffed with nice soft cotton and the hard floor does not bother me at all!" said Raggedy.

At daybreak the next morning Annabel and Thomas awakened to find themselves in Raggedy Ann's bed and as they raised up and looked at each other each knew how ashamed the other felt, for they knew Raggedy Ann had generously given them her bed.

There Raggedy Ann lay; all sprawled out upon the hard floor, her rag arms and legs twisted in ungraceful attitudes.

"How good and honest she looks!" said Annabel. "It must be her shoe-button eyes!"

"How nicely her yarn hair falls in loops over her face!" exclaimed Thomas, "I did not notice how pleasant her face looked last night!"

"The others seem to love her ever and ever so much!" mused Annabel. "It must be because she is so kind."

Both new dolls were silent for a while, thinking deeply.

"How do you feel?" Thomas finally asked.

"Very much ashamed of myself!" answered Annabel, "And you, Thomas?"

"As soon as Raggedy Ann awakens, I shall tell her just how much ashamed I am of myself and if she can, I want her to forgive me!" Thomas said.

"The more I look at her, the better I like her!" said Annabel.

"I am going to kiss her!" said Thomas.

"You'll awaken her if you do!" said Annabel.

But Thomas climbed out of bed and kissed Raggedy Ann on her painted cheek and smoothed her yarn hair from her rag forehead.

And Annabel-Lee climbed out of bed, too, and kissed Raggedy Ann.

Then Thomas and Annabel-Lee gently carried Raggedy Ann and put her in her own bed and tenderly tucked her in, and then took their seats in the two little red chairs.

After a while Annabel said softly to Thomas, "I feel ever and ever so much better and happier!"

"So do I!" Thomas replied. "It's like a whole lot of sunshine coming into a dark room, and I shall always try to keep it there!"

Fido had one fuzzy white ear sticking up over the edge of his basket and he gave his tail a few thumps against his pillow.

Raggedy Ann lay quietly in bed where Thomas and Annabel had tucked her. And as she smiled at the ceiling, her candy heart (with "I LOVE YOU" written on it) thrilled with contentment, for, as you have probably guessed, Raggedy Ann had not been asleep at all!

RAGGEDY ANN
AND THE KITTENS

Raggedy Ann had been away all day.

Marcella had come early in the morning and dressed all the dolls and placed them about the nursery.

Some of the dolls had been put in the little red chairs around the little doll table. There was nothing to eat upon the table except a turkey, a fried egg and an apple, all made of plaster of paris and painted in natural colors. The little teapot and other doll dishes were empty, but Marcella had told them to enjoy their dinner while she was away.

The French dollie had been given a seat upon the doll sofa and Uncle Clem had been placed at the piano.

Marcella picked up Raggedy Ann and carried

her out of the nursery when she left, telling the dolls to "be real good children, while Mamma is away!"

When the door closed, the tin soldier winked at the Dutch-boy doll and handed the imitation turkey to the penny dolls. "Have some nice turkey?" he asked.

"No thank you!" the penny dolls said in little penny-doll, squeaky voices, "We have had all we can eat!"

"Shall I play you a tune?" asked Uncle Clem of the French doll.

At this all the dolls laughed, for Uncle Clem could not begin to play any tune. Raggedy Ann was the only doll who had ever taken lessons, and she could play Peter-Peter-Pumpkin-Eater with one hand.

In fact, Marcella had almost worn out Raggedy Ann's right hand teaching it to her.

"Play something lively!" said the French doll, as she giggled behind her hand, so Uncle Clem began hammering the eight keys on the toy piano with all his might until a noise was heard upon the stairs.

Quick as a wink, all the dolls took the same positions in which they had been placed by Marcella, for they did not wish really truly people to know that they could move about.

But it was only Fido. He put his nose in the door and looked around.

All the dolls at the table looked steadily at the painted food, and Uncle Clem leaned upon the piano keys looking just as unconcerned as when he had been placed there.

Then Fido pushed the door open and came into the nursery wagging his tail.

He walked over to the table and sniffed, in hopes Marcella had given the dolls real food and that some would still be left.

"Where's Raggedy Ann?" Fido asked, when he had satisfied himself that there was no food.

"Mistress took Raggedy Ann and went somewhere!" all the dolls answered in chorus.

"I've found something I must tell Raggedy Ann about!" said Fido, as he scratched his ear.

"Is it a secret?" asked the penny dolls.

"Secret nothing," replied Fido, "It's kittens!"

"How lovely!" cried all the dolls, "Really live kittens?"

"Really live kittens!" replied Fido, "Three little tiny ones, out in the barn!"

"Oh, I wish Raggedy Ann was here!" cried the French doll. "She would know what to do about it!"

"That's why I wanted to see her," said Fido, as he thumped his tail on the floor, "I did not know there were any kittens and I went into the barn to hunt for mice and the first thing I knew Mamma Cat came right at me with her eyes looking green! I tell you I hurried out of there!"

"How did you know there were any kittens then?" asked Uncle Clem.

"I waited around the barn until Mamma Cat went up to the house and then I slipped into the barn again, for I knew there must be something inside or she would not have jumped at me that way! We are always very friendly, you know." Fido continued. "And what was my surprise to find three tiny little kittens in an old basket, 'way back in a dark corner!"

"Go get them, Fido, and bring them up so we can see them!" said the tin soldier.

"Not me!" said Fido, "if I had a suit of tin clothes on like you have I might do it, but you know cats can scratch very hard if they want to!"

"We will tell Raggedy when she comes in!" said the French doll, and Fido went out to play with a neighbor dog.

So when Raggedy Ann had been returned to the nursery the dolls could hardly wait until Marcella had put on their nighties and left them for the night.

Then they told Raggedy Ann all about the kittens.

Raggedy Ann jumped from her bed and ran over to Fido's basket; he wasn't there.

Then Raggedy suggested that all the dolls go out to the barn and see the kittens. This they did easily, for the window was open and it was but a short jump to the ground.

They found Fido out near the barn watching a hole.

"I was afraid something might disturb them," he said, "for Mamma Cat went away about an hour ago."

All the dolls, with Raggedy Ann in the lead, crawled through the hole and ran to the basket.

Just as Raggedy Ann started to pick up one of the kittens there was a lot of howling and yelping and Fido came bounding through the hole with Mamma Cat behind him. When Mamma Cat caught up with Fido he would yelp.

When Fido and Mamma Cat had circled the barn two or three times Fido managed to find the hole and escape to the yard; then Mamma Cat came over to the basket and saw all the dolls.

"I'm s'prised at you, Mamma Cat!" said Raggedy Ann, "Fido has been watching your kittens for an hour while you were away. He wouldn't hurt them for anything!"

"I'm sorry, then," said Mamma Cat.

"You must trust Fido, Mamma Cat!" said Raggedy Ann, "because he loves you and anyone who loves you can be trusted!"

"That's so!" replied Mamma Cat. "Cats love mice, too, and I wish the mice trusted us more!"

The dolls all laughed at this joke.

"Have you told the folks up at the house about your dear little kittens?" Raggedy Ann asked.

"Oh, my, no!" exclaimed Mamma Cat. "At the

last place I lived the people found out about my kittens and do you know, all the kittens disappeared! I intend keeping this a secret!"

"But all the folks at this house are very kindly people and would dearly love your kittens!" cried all the dolls.

"Let's take them right up to the nursery!" said Raggedy Ann, "And Mistress can find them there in the morning!"

"How lovely!" said all the dolls in chorus. "Do, Mamma Cat! Raggedy Ann knows, for she is stuffed with nice clean white cotton and is very wise!"

So after a great deal of persuasion, Mamma Cat finally consented. Raggedy Ann took two of the kittens and carried them to the house while Mamma Cat carried the other.

Raggedy Ann wanted to give the kittens her bed, but Fido, who was anxious to prove his affection, insisted that Mamma Cat and the kittens should have his nice soft basket.

The dolls could hardly sleep that night; they were so anxious to see what Mistress would say when she found the dear little kittens there in Fido's basket next morning.

Raggedy Ann did not sleep a wink, for she shared her bed with Fido and he kept her awake whispering to her.

In the morning when Marcella came to the nursery, the first thing she saw was the three little kittens.

She cried out in delight and carried them all down to show to Mamma and Daddy. Mamma Cat went trailing along, arching her back and purring with pride as she rubbed against all the chairs and doors.

Mamma and Daddy said the kittens could stay in the nursery and belong to Marcella, so Marcella took them back to Fido's basket while she hunted names for them out of a fairy tale book.

Marcella finally decided upon three names; Prince Charming for the white kitty, Cinderella for the Maltese and Princess Golden for the kitty with the yellow stripes.

So that is how the three little kittens came to live in the nursery.

And it all turned out just as Raggedy Ann had said, for her head was stuffed with clean white cotton, and she could think exceedingly wise thoughts.

And Mamma Cat found out that Fido was a very good friend, too. She grew to trust him so much she would even let him help wash the kittens' faces.

RAGGEDY ANN
AND THE FAIRIES' GIFT

All the dolls were tucked snugly in their little doll-beds for the night and the large house was very still.

Every once in a while Fido would raise one ear and partly open one eye, for his keen dog sense seemed to tell him that something was about to happen.

Finally he opened both eyes, sniffed into the air and, getting out of his basket and shaking himself, he trotted across the nursery to Raggedy Ann's bed.

Fido put his cold nose in Raggedy Ann's neck. She raised her head from the little pillow.

"Oh! It's you, Fido!" said Raggedy Ann. "I dreamed the tin soldier put an icicle down my neck!"

"I can't sleep," Fido told Raggedy Ann. "I feel that something is about to happen!"

"You have been eating too many bones lately, Fido, and they keep you awake," Raggedy replied.

"No, it isn't that. I haven't had any bones since the folks had chicken last Sunday. Listen, Raggedy!"

Raggedy Ann listened.

There was a murmur as if someone were singing, far away.

"What is it?" asked Fido.

"Sh!" cautioned Raggedy Ann, "It's music."

It was indeed music, the most beautiful music Raggedy Ann had ever heard.

It grew louder, but still seemed to be *far* away.

Raggedy Ann and Fido could hear it distinctly and it sounded as if hundreds of voices were singing in unison.

"Please don't howl, Fido," Raggedy Ann said as she put her two rag arms around the dog's nose. Fido usually "sang" when he heard music.

But Fido did not sing this time; he was filled with wonder. It seemed as if something very nice was going to happen.

Raggedy Ann sat upright in bed. The room was flooded with a strange, beautiful light and the music came floating in through the nursery window.

Raggedy Ann hopped from her bed and ran across the floor, trailing the bed clothes behind her. Fido followed close behind and together they looked out the window across the flower garden.

There among the flowers were hundreds of tiny beings, some playing on tiny reed instruments and flower horns, while others sang. This was the strange, wonderful music Raggedy and Fido had heard.

"It's the Fairies!" said Raggedy Ann. "To your basket quick, Fido! They are coming this way!" And Raggedy Ann ran back to her bed, with the bed clothes trailing behind her.

Fido gave three jumps and he was in his basket, pretending he was sound asleep, but one little black eye was peeping through a chink in the side.

Raggedy jumped into her bed and pulled the covers to her chin, but her shoe-button eyes could see the window.

Little Fairy forms radiant as silver came flitting into the nursery, singing in far away voices. They carried a little bundle. A beautiful light came from this bundle, and to Raggedy Ann and Fido it seemed like sunshine and moonshine mixed. It was a soft mellow light, just the sort of light you would expect to accompany Fairy Folk.

As Raggedy watched, her candy heart went pitty-pat against her cotton stuffing, for she saw a tiny pink foot sticking out of the bundle of light.

The Fairy troop sailed across the nursery and through the door with their bundle and Raggedy Ann and Fido listened to their far away music as they went down the hall.

Presently the Fairies returned without the bundle and disappeared through the nursery window.

Raggedy Ann and Fido again ran to the window and saw the Fairy troop dancing among the flowers.

The light from the bundle still hung about the nursery and a strange lovely perfume floated about.

When the Fairies' music ceased and they had flown away, Raggedy Ann and Fido returned to Raggedy's bed to think it all out.

When old Mister Sun peeped over the garden

wall and into the nursery, and the other dolls awakened, Raggedy Ann and Fido were still puzzled.

"What is it, Raggedy Ann?" asked the tin soldier and Uncle Clem, in one voice.

Before Raggedy Ann could answer, Marcella came running into the nursery, gathered up all the dolls in her arms, and ran down the hall, Fido jumping beside her and barking shrilly.

"Be quiet!" Marcella said to Fido, "It's asleep and you might awaken it!"

Mamma helped Marcella arrange all the dolls in a circle around the bed so that they could all see what was in the bundle.

Mamma gently pulled back the soft covering and the dolls saw a tiny little fist as pink as coral, a soft little face with a cunning tiny pink nose, and a little head as bald as the French dolly's when her hair came off.

My, how the dollies all chattered when they were once again left alone in the nursery!

"A dear cuddly baby brother for Mistress!"
said Uncle Clem.

"A beautiful bundle of love and Fairy Sun-shine for everybody in the house!" said Raggedy Ann, as she went to the toy piano and joyously played "Peter-Peter-Pumpkin-Eater" with one rag hand.

RAGGEDY ANN
AND THE CHICKENS

When Marcella was called into the house she left
Raggedy sitting on the chicken yard fence. "Now
you sit quietly and do not stir," Marcella told
Raggedy Ann, "If you move you may fall and
hurt yourself!"

So, Raggedy Ann sat quietly, just as Marcella
told her, but she smiled at the chickens for she
had fallen time and again and it had never hurt
her in the least. She was stuffed with nice soft
cotton, you see.

So, there she sat until a tiny little humming-
bird, in search of flower honey hummed close to
Raggedy Ann's head and hovered near the tall
Hollyhocks.

Raggedy Ann turned to see the humming-bird

and lost her balance—*plump!* she went, down amongst the chickens.

The chickens scattered in all directions, all except Old Ironsides, the rooster.

He ruffled his neck feathers and put his head down close to the ground, making a queer whistling noise as he looked fiercely at Raggedy Ann.

But Raggedy Ann only smiled at Old Ironsides, the rooster, and ran her rag hand through her yarn hair for she did not fear him.

Then something strange happened, when she made this motion the old rooster jumped in the air and kicked his feet out in front, knocking Raggedy Ann over and over.

When Raggedy Ann stopped rolling she waved her apron at the rooster and cried, "Shoo!" but instead of "shooing," Old Ironsides upset her again.

Now, two old hens who had been watching the rooster jump at Raggedy ran up and as one old hen placed herself before the rooster, the other old hen caught hold of Raggedy's apron and dragged her into the chicken-coop.

It was dark inside and Raggedy could not tell what was going on as she felt herself being pulled up over the nests.

But, finally Raggedy could sit up, for the old hen had quit pulling her, and as her shoe-button eyes were very good, she soon made out the shape of the old hen in front of her.

"My! that's the hardest work I have done in a long time!" said the old hen, when she could catch her breath. "I was afraid Mr. Rooster would tear your dress!"

"That was a queer game he was playing, Mrs. Hen," said Raggedy Ann.

The old hen chuckled 'way down in her throat, "Gracious me! He wasn't playing a game, he was fighting you!"

"Fighting!" cried Raggedy Ann in surprise.

"Oh yes, indeed!" the old hen answered, "Old Ironsides, the rooster, thought you intended to harm some of the children chickens and he was fighting you!"

"I am sorry that I fell inside the pen, I wouldn't harm anything," Raggedy Ann said.

"If we tell you a secret you must promise not to tell your mistress!" said the old hens.

"I promise! Cross my candy heart!" said Raggedy Ann.

Then the two old hens took Raggedy Ann 'way back in the farthest corner of the chicken coop. There, in back of a box, they had built two nests and each old hen had ten eggs in her nest.

"If your folks hear of it they will take the eggs!" said the hens, "and then we could not raise our families!"

Raggedy Ann felt the eggs and they were nice and warm.

"We just left the nests when you fell into the pen!" explained the old hens.

"But how can the eggs grow if you sit upon them?" said Raggedy. "If Fido sits on any of the garden, the plants will not grow, Mistress says!"

"Eggs are different!" one old hen explained. "In order to make the eggs hatch properly, we must sit on them three weeks and not let them get cold at any time!"

"And at the end of the three weeks do the eggs sprout?" asked Raggedy Ann.

"You must be thinking of eggplant!" cried one old hen. "These eggs hatch at the end of three weeks—they don't sprout—and then we have a lovely family of soft downy chickies to cuddle under our wings and love dearly!"

"Have you been sitting upon the eggs very long?" Raggedy asked.

"Neither one of us has kept track of the time,"

said one hen. "You see, we never leave the nests only just once in a while to get a drink and to eat a little. So we can hardly tell when it is day and when it is night."

"We were going out to get a drink when you fell in the pen!" said one old hen. "Now we will have to sit upon the eggs and warm them up again!"

The two old hens spread their feathers and nestled down upon the nests.

"When you get them good and warm, I would be glad to sit upon the eggs and keep them warm until you get something to eat and drink!" said Raggedy. So the two old hens walked out of the coop to finish their meal which had been interrupted by Raggedy's fall and while they were gone, Raggedy Ann sat quietly upon the warm eggs. Suddenly down beneath her she heard something go, "Pick, pick!" "I hope it isn't a mouse!" Raggedy Ann said to herself, when she felt some-

thing move. "I wish the old hens would come back." But when they came back and saw the puzzled expression on her face, they cried, "What is it?"

Raggedy Ann got to her feet and looked down and there were several little fluffy, cuddly baby chickies, round as little puff-balls.

"Cheep! Cheep! Cheep!" they cried.

"Baby Chicks!" Raggedy cried, as she stooped and picked up one of the little puff-balls.

The two old hens, their eyes shining with happiness, got upon the nests and spread out their soft warm feathers, "The other eggs will hatch soon!" said they.

So, for several days Raggedy helped the two hens hatch out the rest of the chickies and just as they finished, Marcella came inside looking around.

"How in the world did you get in here, Raggedy Ann?" she cried. "I have been looking all about for you! Did the chickens drag you in here?"

Both old hens down behind the box clucked softly to the chickies beneath them and Marcella overheard them.

She lifted the box away and gave a little squeal of surprise and happiness.

"Oh you dear old Hennypennies!" she cried, lifting both old hens from their nests. "You have hidden your nests away back here and now you have one, two, three, four—twenty chickies!" and as she counted them, Marcella placed them in her apron; then catching up Raggedy Ann, she placed her over the new little chickies.

"Come on, old Hennypennies!" she said, and went out of the coop with the two old hens clucking at her heels.

Marcella called Daddy and Daddy rolled two barrels out under one of the trees and made a nice bed in each. Then he nailed slats across the front, leaving a place for a door. Each Hennypennie was then given ten little chickies and shut up in the barrel. And all the dolls were happy when they heard of Raggedy's adventure and they soon were all taken out to see the new chickies.

RAGGEDY ANN AND THE MOUSE

Jeanette was a new wax doll, and like Henny, the Dutch doll, she could say "MAMMA" when anyone tipped her backward or forward. She had lovely golden brown curls of real hair. It could be combed and braided, or curled or fluffed without tangling, and Raggedy Ann was very proud when Jeanette came to live with the dolls.

But now Raggedy Ann was very angry—in fact, Raggedy Ann had just ripped two stitches out of the top of her head when she took her rag hands and pulled her rag face down into a frown (but when she let go of the frown her face stretched right back into her usual cheery smile).

And *you* would have been angry, too, for something had happened to Jeanette.

Something or someone had stolen into the nursery that night when the dolls were asleep and nibbled all the wax from Jeanette's beautiful face—and now all her beauty was gone!

"It really is a shame!" said Raggedy Ann as she put her arms about Jeanette.

"Something must be done about it!" said the French doll as she stamped her little foot.

"If I catch the culprit, I will—well, I don't know what I will do with him!" said the tin soldier, who could be very fierce at times although he was seldom cross.

"Here is the hole he came from!" cried Uncle Clem from the other end of the nursery. "Come, see!"

All the dolls ran to where Uncle Clem was, down on his hands and knees.

"This must be the place!" said Raggedy Ann, "We will plug up the hole with something, so he will not come out again!"

The dolls hunted around and brought rags and pieces of paper and pushed them into the mouse's doorway.

"I thought I heard nibbling last night," one of the penny dolls said. "You know I begged for an extra piece of pie last evening, when Mistress had me at the table and it kept me awake!"

While the dolls were talking, Marcella ran down-stairs with Jeanette and told Daddy and Mamma, who came upstairs with Marcella and hunted around until they discovered the mouse's doorway.

"Oh, why couldn't it have chewed on me?" Raggedy Ann asked herself when she saw Marcella's sorrowful face, for Raggedy Ann was never selfish.

"Daddy will take Jeanette down-town with him and have her fixed up as good as new," said Mamma, so Jeanette was wrapped in soft tissue paper and taken away.

Later in the day Marcella came bouncing into the nursery with a surprise for the dolls. It was a dear fuzzy little kitten.

Marcella introduced the kitten to all the dolls.

"Her name is Boots, because she has four little white feet!" said Marcella. So Boots, the happy little creature, played with the penny dolls, scraping them over the floor and peeping out from behind chairs and pouncing upon them as if they were mice and the penny dolls enjoyed it hugely.

When Marcella was not in the nursery, Raggedy Ann wrestled with Boots and they would roll over and over upon the floor, Boots with her front feet around Raggedy Ann's neck and kicking with her hind feet.

Then Boots would arch her back and pretend she was very angry and walk sideways until she was close to Raggedy. Then she would jump at her and over and over they would roll, their heads hitting the floor bumpity-bump.

Boots slept in the nursery that night and was

lonely for her Mamma, for it was the first time she had been away from home.

Even though her bed was right on top of Raggedy Ann, she could not sleep. But Raggedy Ann was very glad to have Boots sleep with her, even if she was heavy, and when Boots began crying for her Mamma, Raggedy Ann comforted her and soon Boots went to sleep.

One day Jeanette came home. She had a new coating of wax on her face and she was as beautiful as ever.

Now, by this time Boots was one of the family and did not cry at night. Besides Boots was told of the mouse in the corner and how he had eaten Jeanette's wax, so she promised to sleep with one eye open.

Late that night when Boots was the only one awake, out popped a tiny mouse from the hole. Boots jumped after the mouse, and hit against the toy piano and made the keys tinkle so loudly it awakened the dolls.

They ran over to where Boots sat growling with the tiny mouse in her mouth.

My! how the mouse was squeaking!

Raggedy Ann did not like to hear it squeak, but she did not wish Jeanette to have her wax face chewed again, either.

So Raggedy Ann said to the tiny little mouse, "You should have known better than to come here when Boots is with us. Why don't you go out in the barn and live where you will not destroy anything of value?"

"I did not know!" squeaked the little mouse, "This is the very first time in my life that I have ever been here!"

"Aren't you the little mouse who nibbled Jeanette's wax face?" Raggedy Ann asked.

"No!" the little mouse answered, "I was visiting the mice inside the walls and wandered out here to pick up cake crumbs! I have three little baby mice at home down in the barn. I have never nibbled at anyone's wax face!"

"Are you a Mamma mouse?" Uncle Clem asked.

"Yes!" the little mouse squeaked, "and if the kitten will let me go I will run right home to my children and never return again!"

"Let her go, Boots!" the dolls all cried, "She has three little baby mice at home! Please let her go!"

"No, sir!" Boots growled, "This is the first mouse I have ever caught and I will eat her!" At this the little Mamma mouse began squeaking louder than ever.

"If you do not let the Mamma mouse go, Boots, I shall not play with you again!" said Raggedy Ann.

"Raggedy will not play with Boots again!"

said all of the dolls in an awed tone. Not to have Raggedy play with them would have been sad, indeed.

But Boots only growled.

The dolls drew to one side, where Raggedy Ann and Uncle Clem whispered together.

And while they whispered Boots would let the little Mamma mouse run a piece, then she would catch it again and box it about between her paws.

This she did until the poor little Mamma mouse grew so tired it could scarcely run away from Boots.

Boots would let it get almost to the hole in the wall before she would catch it, for she knew it would not escape her.

As she watched the little mouse crawling towards the hole scarcely able to move, Raggedy Ann could not keep the tears from her shoe-button eyes.

Finally as Boots started to spring after the little mouse again, Raggedy Ann threw her rag arms around the kitten's neck. "Run, Mamma mouse!" Raggedy Ann cried, as Boots whirled her over and over.

Uncle Clem ran and pushed the Mamma mouse into the hole and then she was gone.

When Raggedy Ann took her arms from around Boots, the kitten was very angry. She laid her ears back and scratched Raggedy Ann with her claws.

But Raggedy Ann only smiled—it did not hurt her a bit for Raggedy was sewed together with a needle and thread and if that did not hurt, how could the scratch of a kitten? Finally Boots felt ashamed of herself and went over and lay down by the hole in the wall in hopes the mouse would return, but the mouse never returned. Even then Mamma mouse was out in the barn with her children, warning them to beware of kittens and cats.

Raggedy Ann and all the dolls then went to bed and Raggedy had just dozed off to sleep when she felt something jump upon her bed. It was Boots. She felt a warm little pink tongue caress her rag cheek. Raggedy Ann smiled happily to herself, for Boots had curled up on top of Raggedy Ann and was purring herself to sleep.

Then Raggedy Ann knew she had been forgiven for rescuing the Mamma mouse and she smiled herself to sleep and dreamed happily of tomorrow.

RAGGEDY ANN'S NEW SISTERS

Marcella was having a tea party up in the nursery when Daddy called to her, so she left the dollies sitting around the tiny table and ran down stairs carrying Raggedy Ann with her.

Mama, Daddy and a strange man were talking in the living room and Daddy introduced Marcella to the stranger.

The stranger was a large man with kindly eyes and a cheery smile, as pleasant as Raggedy Ann's.

He took Marcella upon his knee and ran his fingers through her curls as he talked to Daddy and Mamma, so, of course, Raggedy Ann liked him from the beginning. "I have two little girls," he told Marcella. "Their names are Virginia and Doris, and one time when we were at the seashore they were playing in the sand and they covered up Freddy, Doris' boy-doll in the sand. They were playing that Freddy was in bathing and that he wanted to be covered with the clean white sand, just as the other bathers did. And when they had covered Freddy they took their little pails and shovels and went farther down the beach to play and forgot all about Freddy.

"Now when it came time for us to go home, Virginia and Doris remembered Freddy and ran down to get him, but the tide had come in and Freddy was 'way out under the water and they could not find him. Virginia and Doris were very sad and they talked of Freddy all the way home."

"It was too bad they forgot Freddy," said Marcella.

"Yes, indeed it was!" the new friend replied as he took Raggedy Ann up and made her dance on Marcella's knee. "But it turned out all right after all, for do you know what happened to Freddy?"

"No, what did happen to him?" Marcella asked.

"Well, first of all, when Freddy was covered with the sand, he enjoyed it immensely. And he did not mind it so much when the tide came up over him, for he felt Virginia and Doris would return and get him.

"But presently Freddy felt the sand above him

121

move as if someone was digging him out. Soon his head was uncovered and he could look right up through the pretty green water, and what do you think was happening? The Tide Fairies were uncovering Freddy!

"When he was completely uncovered, the Tide Fairies swam with Freddy 'way out to the Undertow Fairies. The Undertow Fairies took Freddy and swam with him way out to the Roller Fairies. The Roller Fairies carried Freddy up to the surface and tossed him up to the Spray Fairies who carried him to the Wind Fairies."

"And the Wind Fairies?" Marcella asked breathlessly.

"The Wind Fairies carried Freddy right to our garden and there Virginia and Doris found him, none the worse for his wonderful adventure!"

"Freddy must have enjoyed it and your little girls must have been very glad to get Freddy back again!" said Marcella. "Raggedy Ann went up in the air on the tail of a kite one day and fell, so now I am very careful with her!"

"Would you let me take Raggedy Ann for a few days?" asked the new friend.

Marcella was silent. She liked the stranger friend, but she did not wish to lose Raggedy Ann.

"I will promise to take good care of her and return her in a week. Will you let her go with me, Marcella?"

Marcella finally agreed and when the stranger friend left, he placed Raggedy Ann in his grip.

"It is lonely without Raggedy Ann!" said the dollies each night.

"We miss her happy painted smile and her cheery ways!" they said.

And so the week dragged by. . . .

But, my! What a chatter there was in the nursery the first night after Raggedy Ann returned. All the dolls were so anxious to hug Raggedy Ann they could scarcely wait until Marcella had left them alone.

When they had squeezed Raggedy Ann almost out of shape and she had smoothed out her yarn hair, patted her apron out and felt her shoe-button eyes to see if they were still there, she said, "Well, what have you been doing? Tell me all the news!"

"Oh we have just had the usual tea parties and games!" said the tin soldier. "Tell us about yourself, Raggedy dear, we have missed you so much!"

"Yes! Tell us where you have been and what you have done, Raggedy!" all the dolls cried.

But Raggedy Ann just then noticed that one of the penny dolls had a hand missing.

"How did this happen?" she asked as she picked up the doll.

"I fell off the table and lit upon the tin soldier last night when we were playing. But don't mind

a little thing like that, Raggedy Ann," replied the penny doll. "Tell us of yourself! Have you had a nice time?"

"I shall not tell a thing until your hand is mended!" Raggedy Ann said.

So the Indian ran and brought a bottle of glue. "Where's the hand?" Raggedy asked.

"In my pocket," the penny doll answered.

When Raggedy Ann had glued the penny doll's hand in place and wrapped a rag around it to hold it until the glue dried, she said, "When I tell you of this wonderful adventure, I know you will all feel very happy. It has made me almost burst my stitches with joy."

The dolls all sat upon the floor around Raggedy Ann, the tin soldier with his arm over her shoulder.

"Well, first when I left," said Raggedy Ann, "I was placed in the Stranger Friend's grip. It was rather stuffy in there, but I did not mind it; in fact I believe I must have fallen asleep, for when I awakened I saw the Stranger Friend's hand reaching into the grip. Then he lifted me from the grip and danced me upon his knee. 'What do you think of her?' he said to three other men sitting nearby.

"I was so interested in looking out of the window I did not pay any attention to what they said, for we were on a train and the scenery was just flying by! Then I was put back in the grip.

"When next I was taken from the grip I was in a large, clean, light room and there were many, many girls all dressed in white aprons.

"The stranger friend showed me to another man and to the girls who took off my clothes, cut my seams and took out my cotton. And what do you think! They found my lovely candy heart had not melted at all as I thought. Then they laid me on a table and marked all around my outside edges with a pencil on clean white cloth, and then the girls re-stuffed me and dressed me.

"I stayed in the clean big light room for two or three days and nights and watched my Sisters grow from pieces of cloth into rag dolls just like myself!"

"Your SISTERS!" the dolls all exclaimed in astonishment, "What do you mean, Raggedy?"

"I mean," said Raggedy Ann, "that the Stranger Friend had borrowed me from Marcella so that he could have patterns made from me. And before I left the big clean white room there were hundreds of rag dolls so like me you would not have been able to tell us apart."

"We could have told *you* by your happy smile!" cried the French dollie.

"But all of my sister dolls have smiles just like mine!" replied Raggedy Ann.

"And shoe-button eyes?" the dolls all asked.

"Yes, shoe-button eyes!" Raggedy Ann replied.

"I would tell you from the others by your dress, Raggedy Ann," said the French doll, "Your dress is fifty years old! I could tell you by that!"

"But my new sister rag dolls have dresses just like mine, for the Stranger Friend had cloth made especially for them exactly like mine."

"I know how we could tell you from the other rag dolls, even if you all look exactly alike!" said the Indian doll, who had been thinking for a long time as he sat quietly in his corner.

"How?" asked Raggedy Ann with a laugh.

"By feeling your candy heart! If the doll has a candy heart then it is you, Raggedy Ann!"

Raggedy Ann laughed, "I am so glad you all

love me as you do, but I am sure you would not be able to tell me from my new sisters, except that I am more worn, for each new rag doll has a candy heart, and on it is written, '*I love you*' just as is written on my own candy heart."

"And there are hundreds and hundreds of the new rag dolls?" asked the little penny dolls.

"Hundreds and hundreds of them, all named Raggedy Ann," replied Raggedy.

"Then," said the penny dolls, "we are indeed happy and proud for you! For wherever one of the new Raggedy Ann dolls goes there will go with it the love and happiness that *you* give to others."